Pie in the Sky

ReadZone Books Limited

First published in this edition 2015

© in this edition ReadZone Books Limited 2015
© in text Christine Moorcroft 2010
© in illustrations Stefania Colnaghi 2010

Christine Moorcroft has asserted her right under the Copyright Designs and Patents Act 1988 to be identified as the author of this work.

Stefania Colnaghi has asserted her right under the Copyright Designs and Patents Act 1988 to be identified as the illustrator of this work.

British Library Cataloguing in Publication Data (CIP) is available for this title.

Printed in Malta by Melita Press.

ISBN 978 1 78322 134 9

Visit our website: www.readzonebooks.com

Pie in the Sky

Christine Moorcroft
and Stefania Colnaghi

One fine day, Simon the Pieman and his wife, Myra, went for a ride on their bikes.

Simon had his eyes on the sky.
He spied something shiny
way up high.

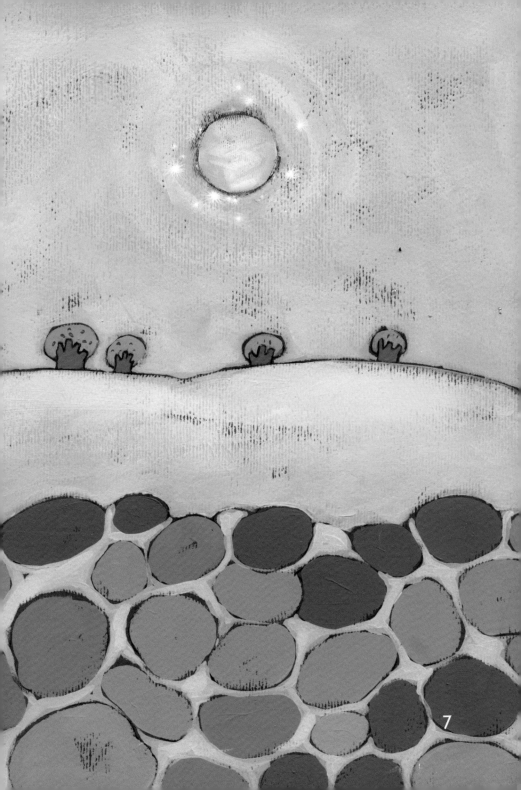

Myra spied it, too. She smiled.
"It's nice and bright."

Simon wiped his eyes.
He was silent for a while.

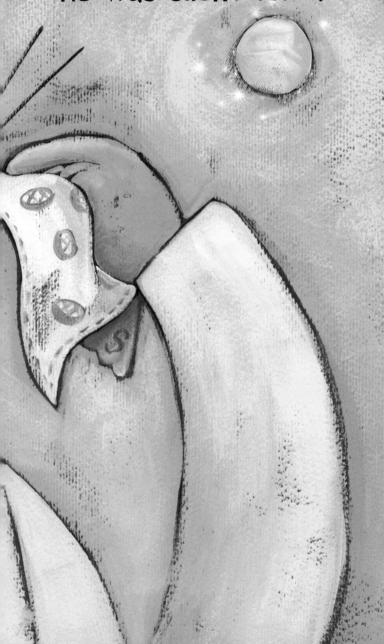

Then he cried,
"I spy a pie – a nice lime pie!"

"Slime pie!" cried Myra.
"How vile."

"Lime, not slime!" said Simon.

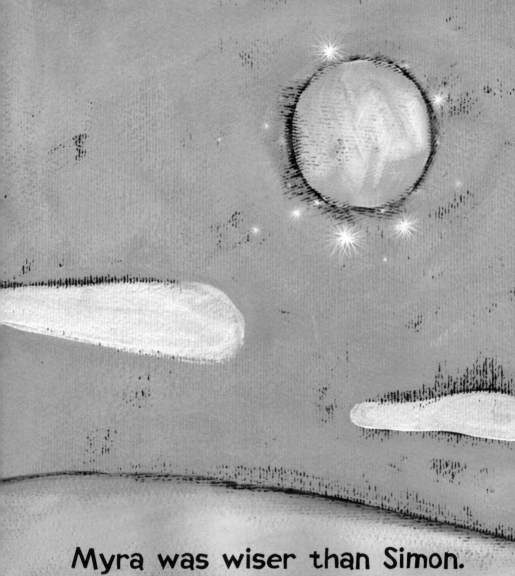

Myra was wiser than Simon.
"No, no. It isn't lime.
It's not a pie!"

17

"By my life, it's a pie,"
said Simon, getting wild.
"I'd like a slice.
Go and find a knife,
wife."

"It's a waste of time to try," replied his wife. "A knife is tiny, the sky is miles high and THERE IS NO PIE!"

Simon decided to stride
away from her side.
He had made up his mind.

"I'm going to climb,"
he said with pride.
"It's worth a try.
The pie will be mine."

Myra tried to hide her smile.
She sat down by a stile
to rest for a while.

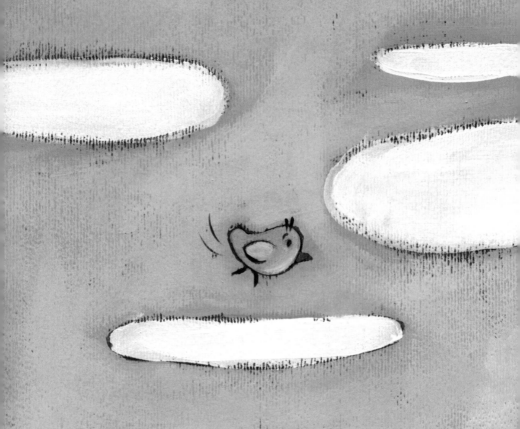

Meanwhile Simon tried and
tried to find the pie.
How did it hide?

29

"Wait until tonight," sighed Myra. "You'll see why there's no pie in the sky.

It's really the moon you silly buffoon."